Small Green Snake

BY LIBBA MOORE GRAY

PICTURES BY
HOLLY MEADE

ORCHARD BOOKS

NEW YORK

Orchard Books
95 Madison Avenue
New York, NY 10016

Manufactured in the United States of America
Printed by Barton Press, Inc.
Bound by Horowitz/Rae
Book design by Sylvia Frezzolini Severance

Hardcover   10 9 8 7 6 5 4 3 2
Paperback   10 9 8 7 6 5 4 3 2 1

The text of this book is set in 16 point Century Schoolbook.
The illustrations are torn paper collage reproduced in full color.

Library of Congress Cataloging-in-Publication Data
Gray, Libba Moore.   Small Green Snake /
by Libba Moore Gray ; illustrated by Holly Meade.
p.   cm.   Summary: Despite his
mother's warning not to wander, Small
Green Snake wiggles away to investigate
the new sound from across the garden wall.
ISBN 0-531-06844-7 (tr.)   ISBN 0-531-08694-1 (lib. bdg.)
ISBN 0-531-07090-5 (pbk.)
[1. Snakes—Fiction.]   I. Meade, Holly, ill.   II. Title.
PZ7.G7793Sm   1994   [E]—dc20   93-49396

For Kylie Elizabeth and John Aubrey
and for Melanie and in memory of
Kelsey Lynne Fleming

—L.M.G.

For the wonderfully curious
and adventurous
Michael Julian Kerr

—H.M.

With a zip and a zag, and a
wiggle and a wag, Small Green Snake
slid down a moss green stone
and startled his mother, who was stretched
out in the grass like a lush lime ribbon.

"I'm a grassy grassy
garter snake
a sassy sassy
flashy flashy
tail twisting
tail turning
tail snapping
green snake
hiss a hiss
a hiss a hiss
a HISSS SSSS ..."

Mama Snake did not smile, for Small Green Snake
had been gone a long time. She raised her long lean
neck and said to him in a stern voice, "Listen, green baby,
if you wander too far you're going to get captured in a
glass jelly jar!"

While his sisters and brother sang in a forked-tongued chorus,

"Uh-huh Uh-huh Uh-huh."

Out flicked Small Green Snake's little black tongue
at them. But when he looked at his mother, he hung
his head and said, "I'll stay in the meadow and listen
for your call, here in the dry grass away from the wall."

So Mama Snake tucked him into a coil for his afternoon nap and stretched out again in hers.

Small Green Snake was almost asleep when—

snippity snippety clippety clippity—

he heard a strange new sound
from across the garden wall.
Up went Small Green Snake's head.
What could it be?

He looked at his mother. She was fast asleep.
He looked at his sisters and his brother.
They were fast asleep, too.

He **curled** and **uncurled,**

did a **flip** and a **flop,**

and out he slid toward the garden wall as fast
as his soft little belly would take him.

ZiP ZiP ZiP

through the hole in the wall
went Small Green Snake,
forgetting all about the promise
he had made to his mother.

"Ah-hah, Ah-hah, Ah-hah,"

sang his sisters and brother
as they watched him disappear.

Oh, Ah-hah!

sang Small Green Snake when
he saw what was on the other
side of the garden wall.
Boldly he slid and sang,

"I'm a grassy grassy
   garter snake
   a sassy sassy
   flashy flashy
   tail twisting
   tail turning
   tail snapping
   green snake. . . ."

right across a big blue shoe.

"Help, help, help!"

squealed the gardener, snapping her
garden shears at him.

"Sorry, sorry, sorry,"

hissed Small Green Snake,
wiggling and waggling away.

Zig, Zag, Zig

raced Small Green Snake. He spotted a coiled green garden hose. It made him think of his mother. Quickly he slid over the coils of plastic and into its center, where he thought he was safe.

"PLIP-PLOP!"

Suddenly Small Green Snake
was trapped—
just as his mother had warned—
in a glass jelly jar.

Poor Small Green Snake.
He was poked and prodded
and turned upside down.
He was shaken and stirred.

By the end of the day he
could hardly wave his tail
or lift his head.
Small Green Snake pressed
his face against the glass.

He missed his mother. He missed his sisters and brother.

rustle
rustle
rustle

went something in the ivy.
Ripple, ripple, roll
went Small Green Snake
as he stretched his lean
green neck in the direction
of the sound.

Suddenly a great ball of orange and white
fluff sailed out of the ivy and . . .
landed on four cat feet, right in front
of Small Green Snake's jar!

Swish swish, swish waved the cat's feathery tail. She stared deep into the narrow black eyes of Small Green Snake.

Snap snap, snap slapped Small Green Snake's tail. He stared back into the eyes of the orange and yellow cat.

Swishedy, swishedy,
snappedy, snappedy.

Wobbledy, wobbledy.

Swish, swish, swish.
Snap, snap, snap.

Wobble, wobble, wobble.
Until . . .

Wheeeeeeee!

went Small Green Snake
as the glass jar went
tipping and turning
down one,
two,
three steps,

landing with a craSh!

Skittery-Scat

went the orange and white cat.

ZiPPedY-ziP

went Small Green Snake.

And with a hiss and a swish he raced across the lawn, through the wall, over a fallen limb, around the ferns and flowers, and into the swaying grass of . . .

Home!

Mama Snake was so happy to have him back that she almost forgot to scold him.

Soon Small Green Snake
had his sisters and brother

crinkling and

wrinkling

in excitement as they listened
to his adventures.

Suddenly they heard a strange new sound—

cha-shsh,
cha-shshsh,
cha-shshshsh,

from across the garden wall.
Up went four green heads.

What could it be?

This time four bobbing heads leaned forward
and four wiggly snakes uncurled in a wavy green line.
And with Small Green Snake leading the way, they sang,

"We're grassy grassy
garter snakes
sassy sassy
flashy flashy
tail twisting
tail turning
tail snapping
green snakes
hiss a hiss a
hiss a hiss a

HISSSSSSSSSS. . . .